MOLLY LIMBO

MOLLY LIMBO

by **Margaret Hodges**

illustrated by **Elizabeth Miles**

Atheneum Books for Young Readers

Author's Note

Many sorts of strange beings, some kind, some mischievous, are described by the English folklorist Katherine Briggs in her *Encyclopedia of Fairies, Hobgoblins, Brownies, Bogies, and Other Supernatural Creatures*. She traces this story back to the seventeenth-century author John Aubrey, who wrote about "Meg Mullack" in his *Miscellanies*. A fuller account is found in Grant Stewart's *Popular Superstitions of the Highlanders of Scotland*, but my version is my own, as is the name, "Molly Limbo."

Atheneum Books for Young Readers
An imprint of Simon & Schuster Children's Publishing Division
1230 Avenue of the Americas
New York, New York 10020

Text copyright © 1996 by Margaret Hodges
Illustrations copyright © 1996 by Elizabeth Miles

Book design by Michael Nelson

The text of this book is set in Adobe Pabst.
The illustrations are rendered in watercolor.

First Edition
Printed in the United States of America
10 9 8 7 6 5 4 3 2 1

Library of Congress Cataloging-in-Publication Data
Hodges, Margaret.
Molly Limbo / by Margaret Hodges ; illustrated by Elizabeth Miles
p. cm.
Summary: When a miserly man buys a supposedly haunted cottage, he discovers that the resident ghost, a pirate's wife, has a sense of fair play.
ISBN 0-689-80581-0
[1. Folklore—England.] I. Miles, Elizabeth, ill. II. Title.
PZ8.1.H69Mo 1996
398.2—dc20
[E] [398.2`094102]
94-3364

For storytellers
—M. H.

For Torsten
—E. M.

There was once a miser named Mr. Means who bought a haunted house. It had been empty for a long time but was fully furnished. Mr. Means did not mind moving in with a ghost if the price was right, and it was. "Besides, I don't believe in ghosts," said Mr. Means.

One room had a big hearth. Here he dug a hole and hid his money boxes under the bricks. "This will be my private room," he said to himself. "No one else will be allowed to come in—no one. But I do need someone to cook and clean."

So he hired a widow who lived in a poor cottage next door and had children to feed. Her name was Mrs. Handy.

"I'll come gladly," she said. "I don't mind the ghost. It's only Molly Limbo. Her husband was a pirate, but she has never been known to do any harm. Besides, she only comes at night when I'll be back in my own house. Now, sir, what about my little ones? In good weather they play in our garden and I can keep an eye on them over the fence. But when it is cold, or rainy, I must bring them with me. If they sit in the kitchen, out of your way, you won't hear a sound from them. I can't leave them at home alone, can I, sir?" said Mrs. Handy.

"I suppose not," said Mr. Means. "How many are there?"

"Only three," said Mrs. Handy. But the next day being sunny, she came alone.

The next day was cold and rainy. Mrs. Handy fed her children and took them into Mr. Means's kitchen by the back door. She put them by the kitchen hearth and said, "Be quiet as mice." Then she picked up her mop and bucket and looked around the house, wondering where to begin work. She looked upstairs and down, into every corner, and could hardly believe her eyes. The windows had been washed, the floors waxed, the furniture polished within an inch of its life.

"Good gracious," she said, "everything is as neat and clean as a new pin. Surely Mr. Means hasn't been doing housework?"

Mr. Means stayed in his own room. He dug up his money boxes, listened to them jingling, and added up figures. At noon he came out, locking the door behind him.

"You need never go into that room. I will clean it myself," he said to Mrs. Handy.

"Indeed I won't, sir," said Mrs. Handy.

Mr. Means then did some business at the bank, and brought home more money. He removed the bricks from his hearth, counted up his new money, and added up more figures. When he shook the boxes, their jingle was music to his ears. But before long he buried the boxes again, locked his door, and went to watch Mrs. Handy at work.

She made him a nice lunch and a supper that he could warm up later. She was an excellent cook. Mr. Means paid her for her day's work.

When she went home that night, she fed her children, watched over their bedtime baths, and tucked them into bed. Then she flopped into her own bed, bone tired.

Mrs. Handy looked about in Mr. Means's house, and rolled up her sleeves. Cobwebs hung in the doorways, and the floors were thick with dust. Mrs. Handy went at her work with a will, but there was much to do. "Almost too much for one person," said Mrs. Handy to herself. "I can't do it all in one day."

At that moment, Mr. Means stormed out of his private room, in a rage. "Mrs. Handy! Mrs. Handy! How did you get into my room? I left it locked, but it has been cleaned! You have stolen my key!"

"Oh, sir, I didn't indeed," cried Mrs. Handy. "Someone else must have been here."

"Who?" Mr. Means snorted. "Who else could get into a locked room?"

Mrs. Handy gasped. "Molly Limbo. She could get through a keyhole. And she has cleaned the whole house. Come and see."

She led Mr. Means through all the rooms. When they went into the kitchen, Mrs. Handy's children were staring at the fire. They seemed to be listening.

"What is it? Do you hear something?" their mother asked.

"Of course. Don't you hear her? It's Molly Limbo, telling us stories."

"Nonsense," said Mr. Means. Then he asked, "Stories? What stories?"

"Ghost stories," said the oldest Handy child. He was eight years old.

"And about pirates," said the second child. She was six.

The youngest child, four years old, said nothing. She was still listening.

"Molly Limbo has never been known to come by day," said Mrs. Handy. "She must have come now to entertain the children. And she has never done any work that I know of. But now she has cleaned the whole house, even the room at the very top. I suppose it's because the house is lived in again."

The oldest Handy child nodded. "That's right. She told us so. Her husband was a pirate. He died a long, long time ago, and she was lonely. The room at the very top is her own room. Shh. She's starting again. I want to listen."

Before she went home that night with her children and her day's wages, Mrs. Handy baked some cupcakes. She left one cake with a mug of milk near the kitchen fire, where Mr. Means saw them before he locked up the house at bedtime.

The next day being sunny, the Handy children played at home in their garden while Mr. Means spoke sternly to Mrs. Handy. "I will not have food left about the house at night. It might attract mice."

"Oh, sir, it was for Molly Limbo," said Mrs. Handy. "See, the mug is empty and the cake is gone. I wanted to thank Molly for her help and hoped she would come again. It's a big house. You really do need two to cook and clean properly, sir."

At noon, when Mrs. Handy opened the oven door to put in a potato for Mr. Means's lunch, she found a loaf of freshly baked bread, brown and crusty, and smelling delicious.

Mr. Means ate most of the bread with a large pat of butter and a pot of tea. He could not help saying, "Excellent bread, Mrs. Handy, excellent."

"Molly Limbo made it," answered Mrs. Handy.

Mr. Means was impressed. "Leave the milk and cake for her again. I don't mind," he said.

And as he paid Mrs. Handy's wages at the end of the day, he thought to himself, Molly Limbo is worthwhile. I still don't believe in her, but if she cooks and cleans, and all for a mug of milk and a cupcake, do I really need Mrs. Handy? No.

The next night he said, "Mrs. Handy, I find I won't be needing you tomorrow. Probably never again. So you had better make other plans."

Mrs. Handy burst into tears. "Oh, sir, hasn't my work pleased you? I have done my best."

"There, there," said Mr. Means. "I'm sure you'll find something else. Here's a little extra money for your trouble."

Mrs. Handy dried her tears and went home. She painted a sign to go in her front window.

STRAWBERRIES
RASPBERRIES
BLACKBERRIES
CIDER IN SEASON

The next morning the Handy children went out into their garden to pick strawberries. It was that season.

But in Mr. Means's house, what a to-do!
He woke to find his trousers on the floor,
turned inside out. The sleeves of his jacket
were tied into tight knots. In the kitchen,
pots and pans had been hurled about, salt
and pepper, sugar, and flour spilled across
the floor. Furniture was turned upside down,
higgledy-piggledy.

In his private room, bricks had been
heaved out of the hearth. Money was
strewn all over the room, and Mr. Means's
business papers had been torn to shreds.

He found rack and ruin in every room·of
the house, except for the room at the very
top. It was perfectly clean. ''Of course,''
said Mr. Means. ''Molly Limbo!''

He ran downstairs where words on the
floury kitchen floor read NOT FAIR TO
MRS. HANDY.

Mr. Means sped out of his house to the fence and leaped over it. Mrs. Handy's kitchen door was open. Her children were eating porridge while she spread honey for them on hot, buttered toast.

"Good morning, Mr. Means," said Mrs. Handy, politely. "What can I do for you?"

Mr. Means was out of breath. "Everything! Everything!" he gasped. "Oh, Mrs. Handy, I have made a terrible mistake. You have no idea what Molly Limbo did last night. Please forgive me and come back. I can even lend a hand myself, if necessary. With the children, I mean. I rather like them, you know. Come to think of it, will you marry me, Mrs. Handy, and become Mrs. Means?"

"Thank you, but no, thank you," said Mrs. Handy. "I have my hands full as it is. But I'll gladly cook and clean for you—if you can manage a small raise in my wages. Molly Limbo will help, I'm sure."

From that time on, Mr. Means's house was always in apple-pie order. His money boxes rested quietly under the hearth in his private room unless he dug them up himself. But he spent less and less time with his business papers and more and more time with Mrs. Handy's children. "Bring them with you, rain or shine," he said. "After all, they are good as gold."

The children's names were Stuart, Drusilla, and Susan. He called them Stue, Drue, and Sue. "And my name is Abigail," said Mrs. Handy. After a while she let him call her Abby.

"My friends used to call me Sam, when I was a boy. It's short for Samson," said Mr. Means. "Please call me Sam."

At night, when the Handy family had gone home, Mr. Means always warmed up the excellent supper that Mrs. Handy had left for him, and ate it sitting by the kitchen fire, looking into the flames. He seemed to be listening.